MARGARET MAHY
Keeping House

Illustrated by
WENDY SMITH

Margaret K. McElderry Books
NEW YORK

W9-AFD-822

The house Lizzie Firkin, the songwriter, lived in was particularly untidy. It was a rough-and-tumble house – unwashed, undusted, and topsy-turvy.

CHADRON STATE COLLEGE

3 9006 00114 5729

M279k

Also by Margaret Mahy for younger children

Nonstop Nonsense
illustrated by Quentin Blake

The Blood-and-Thunder Adventure on
Hurricane Peak
illustrated by Wendy Smith

Making Friends
illustrated by Wendy Smith

(MARGARET K. MCELDERRY BOOKS)

Text copyright © 1991 by Margaret Mahy
Illustrations copyright © 1991 by Wendy Smith

All rights reserved. No part of this book may be reproduced or
transmitted in any form or by any means, electronic or mechanical,
including photocopying, recording, or by any information storage
and retrieval system, without permission in writing from the Publisher.

A Vanessa Hamilton Book
produced in association with Gyldendal, Copenhagen for
Margaret K. McElderry Books
Macmillan Publishing Company
866 Third Avenue
New York, NY 10022

Collier Macmillan Canada, Inc.
1200 Eglinton Avenue East
Suite 200
Don Mills, Ontario M3C 3N1

First Edition

Printed in Portugal
10 9 8 7 6 5 4 3 2 1
CIP is available.

ISBN 0-689-50515-9

Lizzie Firkin couldn't even walk across her own floor because of the mess. She had to jump from one bare spot to another. When she opened the cupboards, a thousand things with sharp corners fell out on top of her. So she nailed the cupboards shut. The cat and the parrot watched her scornfully.

"Don't look at me like that!" Lizzie cried. "I *have* to write songs and practice the trombone."

Every night Lizzie Firkin put on the tights she had painted herself, then – hey ho – off and away she went to a famous nightclub where she sang and tap-danced and played the trombone until the roosters started to crow. It was good fun.

But playing the trombone every night always made Lizzie Firkin too tired to sweep away dust and cobwebs, to pick up anything off the floor, or to tidy the cupboards.

"I'm quite worn out," she told the cat and the parrot one day.
"The house is so topsy-turvy that I've decided to send for Robin
Puckertucker, the Wonder Housekeeper."

She looked up the number and telephoned immediately.

"This is a recorded message," said a voice. "Robin Puckertucker is out
cleaning houses, trying to make a fortune. Please leave your name and
address when you hear the tone and Robin will rush 'round early
tomorrow morning. And please make sure you don't spoil things by
trying to tidy up yourself!"

No fear of that, thought Lizzie Firkin, recording her name and address on the answering machine.

She did an hour's trombone practice, dyed her hair red, painted a few extra designs on her clothes, then – hey ho – off and away she went to the famous nightclub, where she danced and sang and played the trombone until the roosters started to crow.

Lizzie Firkin came home very late, as usual. She switched on the light, as usual, and blinked at her untidy house, as usual. Unsuccessful songs lay scattered like autumn leaves over the floor. The cat was curled up in the breadbox, asleep on the sliced bread. The parrot was molting.

The vacuum cleaner sulked under the stairs, its cord·wound sadly
around itself, like a dog that has given up hope of ever being taken for a
walk. Bottles of hair dye stood shoulder to shoulder, like soldiers, on top
of the piano.

"Oh dear!" exclaimed Lizzie Firkin. "How messy it all is. What will Robin Puckertucker think of the cat asleep in the breadbox? Or of all those parrot feathers? I'd better tidy up – just a little bit – so the Wonder Housekeeper won't know how terribly untidy I really am."

"Horrakapotchkin!" cried Robin Puckertucker in despair to the parrot. "They all send for me, and then they become scared that I will find out how messy they really are and tidy everything up themselves. I'll never make a fortune if things go on like this. But why," he asked curiously, "are the cupboards all nailed shut?"

But Lizzie Firkin did not answer. She was already sound asleep in her chair, snoring musically and dreaming of trombones.

"I am Robin Puckertucker," replied the young man, gazing around him. Then, sounding distinctly disappointed, he added, "What a particularly tidy house you have. Alas, there is nothing left for me to do!"

"Are you the trombone player who is particularly untidy at home?" he asked, looking around in astonishment.

And no wonder he was taken aback. Lizzie Firkin's house sparkled from the front door to the back door. It shone from ceiling to floor. The cat purred; even the parrot looked smartly groomed.

"And who are you?" asked Lizzie Firkin, too tired to be surprised.

Out by the gate the grandfather clock struck nine. In bounded a dashing young man wearing an apron with a smile painted on it.

RETA E. KING LIBRARY
CHADRON STATE COLLEGE
CHADRON, NE 00000

"I mustn't let Robin Puckertucker know how untidy I really am," she muttered as she shook the crumbs off the cat, dusted the parrot, put the grandfather clock out by the gate, and wound up the garbage pail. Then she tumbled into her big chair – quite, quite exhausted.

By now the sun was looking over the hill. It showed up every spot on the windows, every cobweb on the curtains, and every smear on the floor. Lizzie Firkin yawned so hard that she nearly sucked the parrot off his perch. But she polished the floor, washed the windows, and brushed away the cobwebs. The spiders packed their bags and moved to the house next door. Lizzie's eyes were almost shut, and she could not stop yawning.

washed the dishes,

wiped the table,

cleaned the bathtub,

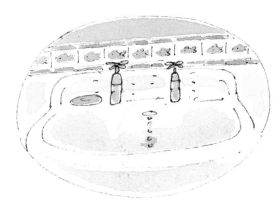

polished the faucets
until they sparkled,

and threw out the stale soup
in the refrigerator.

"Good, but not quite good enough," she said, and yawned. "Robin Puckertucker must never know just how untidy I can be. The shock might kill a good housekeeper."

Lizzie picked up all
the newspapers

and folded them carefully.

She vacuumed the floor,

dusted the piano,

shined up her trombone,

Lizzie shooed the cat out of
the breadbox.

She picked up the unsuccessful
songs and put them
in a folder.

She tossed the empty
cat-food cans into
the garbage pail.

The roosters were still crowing when she
stopped and looked around.

Snatching up the soup ladle, he pried open a door that had been nailed shut for three years. A thousand things with sharp corners fell on top of him.

"Oh joy! Housework at last!" Robin Puckertucker cried faintly but happily from the bottom of the pile. "I shall insist on everyone opening their cupboards from now on, and I shall make a fortune after all!"